Tales from Clear Creek

Walt Ryan

Illustrations by Tom Runnels
and Walt Ryan

Copyright © 2014 Walt Ryan
All rights reserved.

ISBN: 0990636607
ISBN-13: 978-0-9906366-0-1

This book is dedicated to:

My artist friend from Marble Hill, Missouri,
the late Tom Runnels.
I would send Tom a draft and he would send back a drawing
that always caught the essence of the story.

And to my childhood hunting and Oak Ridge school buddy,
the late Richard Jackson from the Portia, Missouri community.

CONTENTS

The Coon Hunt	1
First Horse	9
Groundhogs are Good Eating	14
Coyote Run	19
The Bobcat	24
A Close Call	30
The Town Kids	33
Who Believes a Kid?	36
Watermelon and a Good Cigar	42
The Open Well	48
Midnight Saves a Jersey	50
The Mailman's Lecture	54
The Day I Heard Joe Swear	60
Home Again Safe and Sound	63
Author's Notes	67

The Coon Hunt

I opened my eyes and lay there in the dark, wondering what had awakened me. Then it came again, a peck on the window and someone called my name.

"It's me. Are you there?"

"I'm here, Rich," I answered. "Hey, where were you last evening? I thought we were going to take those pups out last night."

"Yeah, well, I had some problems with my chores," he said. "Mom said I couldn't go hunting last evening. It's after two o'clock now and she didn't say any thing about this morning! What you say, let's go? I've got the dogs tied to the fence down by the road," he added.

This sounded logical to me. "Just a minute, I'll get dressed," I said.

"Bring your rifle," he hissed through the window. "I couldn't get my stuff together without waking somebody up."

I dressed hurriedly, retrieving my treasured hand-me-down hunting boots from beneath the bed. I dipped into my precious cache of .22 shorts and dropped a handful into the pocket of my denim chore coat.

Picking up the old Winchester from beside the back door, I slipped out into the cool November night, joining Richard. At the barn, we added a kerosene lantern and a gunny sack to our gear and started across the pasture to the dogs.

Richard and I lived in a small farming community in southwest Missouri. He was a few years younger than me. We attended a one room country school during the early 1950's. We became hunting buddies and each hunting trip was an adventure. This early morning coon hunt wouldn't be an exception.

The dogs bawled out their displeasure at being tied. They were pups just out of the awkward stage, mostly feet, ears and enthusiasm. A Black and Tan and a Bluetick, they had the makings of good dogs. They had been out a time or two. Just enough experience to know what it was about.

We untied the pups and started across the field to a timbered draw that led down to the Clear Creek bottoms. When we reached the draw we stopped on the outskirts of the timber. Taking a match from the battered Doans pillbox in my pocket, I lit the lantern.

There was a movement at the edge of the circle of lantern light. Rich said, "That mutt of yours has followed us. I don't want him throwing my coon hounds off. Send him back."

My dog was a mutt. He was a mixture. With a bulldog build and spaniel head and coat, he didn't look like a hunting dog, but he was an excellent squirrel and rabbit dog. He was also fearless. He would tackle anything from a copperhead snake to a coyote.

"Pretty good possum dog," I muttered.

"Don't care," he said. "My dogs don't tree possum. He's liable to get them doing things they ought not to do."

Rich was right, he didn't belong on a coon hunt. I pulled a weed for a switch and ran the dog back towards the house, admonishing him to stay home.

The hounds dropped into the draw and ranged ahead. We followed along the upper edge where the walking was easy. We could hear them as they foraged around in the leaves looking for a scent.

Suddenly one hound sounded a discovery and down toward the creek they went. "That's the Bluetick, he's tracking," Rich boasted. We made our way down onto the floor of the draw and started after the dogs at a trot.

We found them at the base of an old water oak with numerous branches draped in wild grapevines. "There is a coon up there," Rich said.

"I don't know," I answered. "They aren't very excited about him, if it is." I held the lantern high, hoping to pick up a shine on the eyes. "OK, I see him!" I shouted.

Holding the lantern up in one hand, I laid the .22 over a sapling limb, hooked the butt into my shoulder, aimed at the eyes, and touched off a shot. It dropped through the branches and hung up in the vines about six feet above the ground. "I got him. It's a possum," I said.

"No. You didn't," Rich argued, "he's still up there." As if to add credence to his master, the Black and Tan stretched up on the tree trunk and bawled skyward for all he was worth.

I circled around with the lantern and soon I could see a second furry form not too far up in the tree. Rich held the lantern up and I shot that one out. It was another possum.

We dropped our bounty in the sack, called to the dogs and started on down the creek. Rich was suddenly devoid of conversation and I decided not to mention the possums that were supposed to be raccoons. He carried the sack and I carried the rifle and the lantern. We trudged on, each with our own thoughts.

Suddenly both dogs opened up and lined out on track

at full cry. It was beautiful music to our ears and we stopped to listen. My pulse quickened in expectation of a quick tree.

It didn't happen. The quarry was running. "They're running a deer," I offered.

"Baloney," Rich said. "It's an old ridge coon, they don't tree. They live in holes in the ground." Then the dogs caught their quarry and the sounds of a fight reached us. We started in the direction of the chase, pausing occasionally to listen.

They were off and running again. "Could be a bobcat," I mused. "They're across the creek and I've seen cat sign over there." Rich took off running like the devil was after him.

"We got to get to them! If it's a bobcat, it will tear those pups up!" he yelled back. "There's a log across the creek down here somewhere," he added.

We hit the log on the run, Rich first. About two-thirds of the way across, it dumped us. Rich landed on his hands and knees in shallow water. I managed to stay upright in water waist deep. The lantern got wet and went out.

We waded out and I tried to dry the lantern out, thankful that the pillbox kept the matches dry. The wick finally caught fire and we started out at a fast clip.

The dogs went back across the creek again and treed. The sharp yip-yip of my mutt could be heard right along with the hounds. He had joined the chase. Rich didn't protest this time.

"How are we going to get back across?" Rich panted.

"The railroad bridge," I answered. "They are over northwest of it now." High above Clear Creek, the railroad trestle was a challenge in daylight. In the dark we threw caution aside and took to it at full speed, hitting every third cross member.

"It's jumped out. They're running again," Rich called out. In a few minutes he added, "They are on the ridge west of Todd's Ford."

They caught their prey again and the battle raged. We charged on down the wagon road then through the sassafras sprouts and back across to the railroad tracks. The sounds of the struggle grew closer and every now and then one of the hounds would yelp in pain.

Winded and fearful, we climbed the hill and arrived at the battle scene.

The pups were out of the fight, tuckered out with tongues lolling and sides heaving. Both were marked and bloodied. The Black and Tan was missing a piece of one ear.

The mutt was locked in a to-the-death struggle with an old coon as big as he was.

"Shoot him!!" Rich screamed. "He's gonna kill your dog! Shoot him!"

"I can't, I'm liable to hit the dog," I said, dancing around looking for an opening.

Rich, always the man of action, grabbed a club. Wading

into the melee, he pounded them apart. The coon ran into the clear and I dispatched him with the .22.

He was the largest coon we had seen. He was old and mean. Rather than tree, he had elected to fight the green pups.

"Yup," Rich said. "It is just like I said before, an old ridge coon." Rich added him to the sack. "They done good didn't they?" he said.

"Yep, those pups are gonna make some top coon dogs," I answered.

"Yes sir, they all done good," he added, giving the mutt his due.

We started for home and the dogs were content to follow us. "What do you think that old coon will weigh?" Rich asked.

"He's as big as they come. Perhaps 25 pounds," I ventured.

"Nope, closer to 20, I figure," he said. We didn't have access to scales and no way to prove our guesses, but we argued anyway. After awhile we grew weary of it and ceased talking for a half mile or so.

"I just got my F.C. Taylor price list a few days ago," I noted. "Possum hides are still fifty cents each. That's a box of shells," I continued. "Coon hides are gonna fetch up to five dollars, if they're good and prime." Silence again. The excitement and the exertion were beginning to tell on us.

The sun was just peeking above the horizon when we

reached the lower lot fence. As we turned toward the barn, we could hear old Mr. Hicks on down the road, calling his cows. Somewhere a rooster crowed.

"Hey, wasn't that a race?" he asked.

"Yup sure was. The best I ever had," I answered.

"Yes sir," he said. "We got to do that again, soon!"

First Horse

He was just a weanling colt. We bought him at an auction. I rode home in the pickup truck with him. I wrapped my arms around his neck, and talked to him to reassure him. We had other horses, but this one would be mine to break, to train, and ride.

The months went by. He learned to trust me. He let me handle his feet. He grew accustomed to the halter, saddle, and then the bridle. We trekked all over the place. The colt followed me decked out in full riding gear.

We were buddies. He thought he was my peer, my equal. He was a pet and that would cause him to be more difficult to break. I knew I must ride him soon before he grew older and stronger. It took a long time for me to work up the nerve to make that first ride.

Finally it was time. I led him out into the middle of the hay meadow. I fussed with the tack, tightening the cinch on the old rodeo association regulation tree saddle. Made by the Gallup saddle makers of Pueblo, Colorado, it was a splendid, all-around, old-time, working saddle. I figured that once I was firmly anchored in the deep seat, I could ride him out.

I caught my breath, turned the stirrup out, shoved my foot in, and swung on. I hooked the off stirrup and settled in. I had my firm seat.

He turned his head to size up what was happening. I clicked my tongue and nudged him with my right foot. He stepped out, got his head down, and started to buck.

He made several short bone-jarring jumps. Then he bucked sideways. I lost a stirrup, then regained it. It seemed like an eternity. The border fence loomed up beside us. A barb on the top wire caught my pants leg and ripped a hole. I bailed off, fearing injury to the horse or myself.

My knees were weak. I leaned against him, letting him calm down. I let him blow, building up my nerve. I knew I couldn't stop. I had to finish the job. Finally I led him back out into the meadow.

    I stroked his shoulder and talked to him, taking the reins up in my left hand. Mounting up, I kept a tight rein, holding his head up this time.

    He began to run. When he started toward the fence, I turned him by pulling his head around. He ran the full length of the meadow and then back again.

    He was larger and stronger, but I stayed with him. Out there in the meadow we finally came to terms. I would ride and he would carry. A partnership began that was to last many years. He never bucked again.

    His training progressed nicely. He learned to work cattle. We drove them from pasture to pasture or to the barn lot. Nothing fancy was needed, our stock was a mixture of dairy and beef. Dad had given me orders to go easy on the dairy stock.

    I decided to train him with the rope. After all, every good stock horse should know how to work under a rope. I started by dropping loops over fence posts. Then I secured the rope to the saddle horn. I would get off and make him back off to tighten the slack. I would jerk and tug on the rope. He would face me and set back on it like a pro.

    I shook a loop out, and twirled it around his ears and across his rump, time after time. I would ride alongside and pop the flies off the cows with the loop just to keep him familiar with the rope...

Several weeks later, we were bringing some yearling heifers up from the pasture. The small herd consisted of some Shorthorn and some Jerseys. One of the Jerseys was a little roguish. She had a perfect picture book set of small horns. In fact, she looked just like the picture that we used to see on the condensed milk can.

The cows were filing through the gate when the Jersey decided to make a break for it. The horse wheeled and went after her on his own, but she had a lead on us and was about to get away. In frustration, I flipped the loop after her.

Then things started to happen. The loop floated out over her back and settled perfectly over her horns. The horse went into a slide, throwing his weight to his rear legs. He was as solid as an oak tree when the heifer hit the end of the rope. She went airborne, turning a cartwheel through the air and landed on her side with a sickening thud.

I jumped off the horse and raced to the heifer thinking I had killed her. I jerked the loop off her horns and she just laid there groaning with her eyes rolled back in her head. I nudged her with the toe of my boot. To my relief she finally scrambled up and trotted towards the gate.

I coiled the rope and started to get back on the horse. Looking toward the barn, I saw my Dad standing in the doorway. "Bring it here," he said. Head down, I shuffled over and reluctantly handed the rope to him.

The rope disappeared for several weeks and then one day it suddenly appeared on a nail in the feed alley. I watched it for several days. Finally, I slipped it down and tied it back on the saddle. The horse and I were back in business. I never had anymore trouble from that heifer. She knew I could reach out and touch her!

Groundhogs Are Good Eating

The kitchen screen door slammed shut behind me with a crack that broke into the early morning stillness. The dog come racing around the corner of the house, with breakfast table scraps on his mind. I sat down on the sandstone step. Pulling the loading tube out of the old Winchester, I fed a dozen .22 long rifle shells into the magazine. The dog began to dance around in eager anticipation. He knew that when the rifle came out, a hunting trip was in the making.

We headed south across the pasture, then angled east down the slope to the edge of the timber, just in case an early morning squirrel got careless.

The sun was burning away the last few low pockets of fog. We moved on briskly with a purpose. And we did have a purpose. A few days before, my dad had toured the Clear Creek bottom cornfields and found that the groundhogs were working on the corn. They were riding the stalks down and chewing, or carrying off the tender young ears of corn.

Dad issued me a new box of .22 long rifle shells and instructed me to thin the groundhogs out. The dog and I were going about our assignment in earnest.

We crawled through the pasture fence and came out onto the rocky roadbed. The dog uttered a low growl. He raised his hackles, alerting me that someone or something was nearby.

Looking ahead, I spotted old Mr. Todd standing under the old oak tree beside the drive into the old house at the crown of the hill. He was leaning against the hickory stick he used for a walking staff. I could just make him out in the morning fog.

Mr. Todd was an interesting person, but different. He lived alone without even a dog to keep him company. His home was a two room dilapidated shack on a ridge above Clear Creek near the Katy (M.K.T.) railroad tracks. He owned a considerable chunk of land along the creek. The deteriorated barns and pen fences attested to the fact that at one time he had raised a lot of livestock.

He was an intelligent man of measured and dignified speech. I visited him several times at his cabin. It was cluttered and filled with remnants of the past. He hung each year's calendar over the last one, driving a new nail and starting over when that nail filled up. He had calendars dating back into the 1920's. My favorite was the one with an artist's version of a pretty Indian girl complete with buckskins, beads, and feathered headband!

He stored his sack of flour and a side of bacon on his heating stove to keep them out of reach of vermin. Each metal leg of the stove was sitting in an open salmon tin partially filled with motor oil. I always wondered where he stored his flour and bacon in the winter...

"Good morning, Mr. Todd," I said.

"Hello Walter, you are out early this morning," he replied.

"Yes sir, we are going hunting. Groundhog hunting. They are pulling the corn down and eating the ears. They really like it when it gets to roasting ear stage."

"I see," he said. Eyeing the dog, he added, "I knew he was a squirrel dog, but I did not know he was a groundhog hunter, too. A groundhog is almost as large as he is. How does he work?"

"Well we hide in the weeds and wait until the groundhog shows up and when I shoot it, the dog runs out and makes sure it is dead. He gets kind of mad when I miss."

"Oh, you miss, do you?"

"Yep, miss every once in a while. They are tricky varmints to hit."

"Yes, they are a remarkable animal. They are strict vegetarians you know. Fact is, groundhogs are good eating."

"I don't care to eat them myself," I said. Quickly I added, "I will bring you one if you wish?"

"I would not mind having a nice fat young one," the old gent said.

"Well, I got to be going. I will bring you one if I get a

young one," I promised.

A few days later we got our chance at a young one... Hiding in the weeds near the Indian Tree between the corn and Clear Creek, I spied a half-grown groundhog making his way up an outside row of corn. The rifle cracked and the dog went out to claim the prize.

We cut across the bottoms coming out at Mr. Todd's gate just above the railroad tracks. We followed the wagon road along the ridge and found the old man standing at the well by his cabin.

"Hello Walter. What have we here? You sure enough found a young one." He took the field-dressed carcass and laid it on the well platform. He reached deep into the right pocket of his overalls and produced a quarter. "Here," he said. "Will this be enough for your trouble?"

"Yes Sir, thanks." A quarter was half the price of a box of .22 shorts. I could see a profitable business developing. "Do you reckon you will be needin' another one?"

A look of amusement crossed the old man's face. "No, I think this one will do for this year at least, but thanks for asking."

I used to go back and quail hunt once in a while. The Bobwhite quail were thick in the overgrown pasture west of his cabin. It has been fifty years now since I have been to the Clear Creek bottoms. I know Bud Todd's old cabin and the giant walnut trees that harbored so many squirrels are long gone. The railroad is gone. Just maybe the blackberries, the wild goose berries, and the sassafras remain. But, the memories are here. The memories of a boy and his dog growing up on a hardscrabble farm near the Clear Creek bottoms.

Coyote Run

Located across the road from a grain elevator and feed store, it was a typical farm community gas station. It was a good place to sit and visit while your car or truck was serviced. I had worked there, when a teenager.

I stepped through the door and saw him sitting on one of the benches along the wall. "Hi," he said, "do you know me?"

"Yes," I answered, saying his name. He was a farmer from the Filley community. I remembered that he had kept a good pack of running dogs through the years.

"Do you still own that little bay horse?" he asked.

It had been a long time since I owned that horse. "No, I sold him to Earl Powers when I came home on leave from basic training several years ago. He wanted him for his grandchildren. The horse is way up in his twenties now." I continued, "I have heard that he is still toting kids around."

"Boy that horse could run," he said. "I will never forget that run you made chasing that coyote."

I was at once embarrassed and a mite cautious. Coyote hunters typically did not appreciate someone jumping ahead of their running dogs. I knew that and had known that at the time he spoke of, even if I was just a boy in my early teens.

"Yes," I said a bit uneasily. "The horse was all heart and I was pretty reckless." I sat down beside him and we chatted. We talked of the horse and that coyote chase of a long time ago.

The horse was a Quarter Horse mix. He was a weanling when we bought him at an auction. I broke him to ride and trained him on my own. We grew up together. The horse was both friend and transportation for a 50's era hardscrabble farm boy. He was a small horse, only a little over fourteen hands tall. He was surefooted and he would try about anything I asked him to do. We rambled and hunted all over the prairie hills and creek bottoms. Shooting the rifle from his back was almost as easy as shooting from a ground position. He was that steady.

That particular Saturday morning started out innocent enough. I saddled up after the chores were finished, and we ambled down through the bottom road. I balanced the .22 in my lap against the fork of the saddle and scanned the treetops for a careless squirrel.

We turned off the road into a large open field with a thick cover of weeds. I intended to check some likely-looking squirrel timber at the far end. I could hear some dogs tracking in the distance. They were coming toward us and getting closer. I figured they were running a coyote. Coyotes were plentiful, as evidenced by the way they were working on our chickens.

The horse snorted and started stepping sideways. The coyote came up out of the weeds right in front of us. He cut to my left. I slammed a shot at him and missed. He was headed for the stone fence at the edge of the field. The horse steadied and I shot again just as the coyote jumped the fence. I saw a piece of fur fly from over his shoulders and he was gone.

The horse wheeled around and we headed for the fence. We cleared it at the same spot the coyote did. I caught a flash of movement and picked out the coyote running through the timber. We followed him up the draw and into the road. He was covering ground fast and I knew I hadn't hurt him much.

At the turn in the road the coyote went up the road

bank and through the barbed wire fence. The horse knew he couldn't make that fence and stopped. I watched the coyote run north into a stand of timber. That patch of timberland had been grazed pretty heavily. I knew there wouldn't be enough cover for him in there. He was traveling north and I figured he would come out on the north end of the timber. There was open prairie there, tall grass interspersed with patches of buck brush and shallow ditches. It would give him the cover he wanted.

I turned the horse north up the dirt road and asked him to run. He stretched out and gave it all he had. At a rise in the road the timber gave way to open prairie. We jumped the road ditch and whipped out into the grass.

Hoping that we were ahead of him, I stopped to watch and listen. I could hear the dogs barking on our distant back trail. The hunter's pickup was coming slowly over the road behind me.

Suddenly the coyote broke out of the timber and headed across the prairie field. He was just out of range and I charged him in an attempt to narrow the distance for a killing shot.

He was still running well and we were at it again, breakneck across the meadow. He angled back toward the road and a heavy multiflora rose fence. The horse cut across the corner of the meadow and jumped a couple of ditches in a vain attempt to head the coyote off. The coyote made it through the fence, and I couldn't touch him with the .22.

I started the horse down and around the fence expecting to catch the coyote coming up the other side. He beat us back to the road and I saw him cross it.

Another pickup with dogs and hunters were approaching on the road from the north and those hunters saw him, too. Quickly, they released a fresh pack of hounds. Not wanting a confrontation, I pulled up and watched from a distance. The hunters waved a greeting. I waved back and turned the horse towards home, giving up a lost cause...

"What happened to the coyote?" I asked.

"The fresh dogs cornered him about a half mile further on. You marked him. If you would have been shooting a larger gun, you would have knocked him down.

Then he said again, "Boy, what a chase. That horse could run!"

The Bobcat

It was evening. We sat out in the yard enjoying the cool refreshing night air, gaining a little respite from the Southwest Missouri summer heat. The conversation had ceased.

The sound drifted up from the creek bottom fields, startling us out of our thoughts. It was an eerie sound, once, and then again. It sounded like a woman's scream. My mind's eye was instantly filled with visions of a mountain lion.

My Granddad Cole had visited a few weeks before. As always, he had entertained us with stories. This time he had told of mountain lion hunts in New Mexico. He claimed when they screamed, they sounded like a woman in distress.

"It's a panther," I said.

"What is it John?" my mother asked my father, ignoring me.

"Probably a screech owl or loon, maybe a bobcat," he answered.

We heard it again a few nights later. My curiosity couldn't be contained. I started to search for the panther, bobcat, or whatever. My family laughed at me. My mother worried about my overactive imagination.

The truth is, good habitat for bobcats abounded along Clear Creek. During the post World War II years, many of the old farms along the bottoms had been abandoned. They became property of out-of-the-area owners and were allowed to grow over with weeds and sprouts.

Through the efforts of the Missouri Conservation Commission, even a few deer began to show up along the Clear Creek bottoms. I was young, but with the research I had done and my grandfather's stories, I knew that larger predators would be attracted by the deer.

First, I checked the banks of Clear Creek. I figured that sometime or other, a cat would leave tracks in the mud. I was right. After several weekends of tramping along the creek, I found the sign I was looking for. The tracks were perhaps as large as a dog or coyote but not large enough to belong to a panther. There were no claw marks. They had to be pug marks left by a bobcat.

I rushed home with news of my find. My dad didn't share my excitement. "They're just overgrown bob-tailed house cats," he said. Now that I had maybe solved the mystery of the eerie sounds he wanted me to forget about it. There were more important things to attend to. Like chores.

I couldn't put the bobcat out of my mind. At the public library I researched all the information I could find on bobcats. Returning to the Clear Creek bottoms I found more tracks, partially covered feces, and scattered fur and blood from rabbit kills. I narrowed my stalking area down to a heavily timbered area. The timber was interspersed with thick underbrush, bordered by tall grasses and briars with an open field to the west. The creek ran through it all.

I bought a box of .22 long rifle hollow points. Shorts would not do. I was hunting big game. I spent hours moving through the area. I would creep along, stopping to stand for minutes at a time.

Changing my tactics, I left at daybreak one Saturday hoping to catch some early morning movement in the woods. Arriving in the creek bottom, I found that the lingering fog obscured the whole valley. Picking a spot on the south side of an old rock fence, I sat down to wait for the sun to burn the fog away. I sat there waiting and watching. Then I heard a noise from behind the fence.

At first it was just a scratching noise and then unmistakably the sound of an animal eating. Crunch, crunch. Was it a coyote or a bobcat devouring a rabbit? I turned my head slightly, trying to see between the rocks in the fence. I was in a predicament. If I peeked over I would surely give myself away.

I did not know the animal's exact location. Slowly, I gathered my legs under me and prepared to jump the fence. I counted to three and went over. I landed on one knee with the rifle in shooting position. About fifteen feet in front of me a mama skunk and four or five young ones (I did not take time to count them) were eating grubs and beetles they had found in the rotted remains of an old log.

The old skunk charged for a few feet with her teeth clicking. Then she turned her rear end toward me and did a hand stand. I hurled myself back over the rock fence. I scrambled to my feet and put at least fifty yards between me and the skunk family before I even looked back.

Time wore on, but I did not give up. I knew they were there. Sometime I would see a bobcat...

It was early fall now. The crops were out and it was my assignment to check the fences before we let the cattle in to graze down the corn and soybean stubble. I had started home, coming out of the timber to the edge of the field for easier walking. As I trudged along, I happened to look to my right at an old windfall a few yards back in the timber. The tree had been there for several years, the trunk parallel with the ground.

It was standing on the tree trunk looking straight at me. The eyes were large and yellow. The ears tufted. The tawny mottled coat was beautiful. In a split second the cat was gone.

I had to have that pelt. I had to get that cat. It had tested my skill as a woodsman and it had bested me. Now I knew what I would do. I would trap it. I reasoned and rightly so, that bobcats were creatures of habit. Sooner or later it would visit the windfall again and I would trap it.

Following good trap-setting procedures, I carefully set a trap in a shallow hole a few feet out from the end of the log. Taking care not to touch ground near the trap set with anything but my rubber boots and gloves, I drove the trap stake in the hole. Then I depressed the spring and set the trigger. Leaves and a light sifting of loose dirt finished the camouflage. I just knew the cat would jump from the end of the log sometime…

I checked the trap mostly from the back of the horse. Riding up to within a hundred yards or so I would stand up in the stirrups and survey the trap location without leaving a bit of scent. It had been early fall when the trap was set. Now early winter, the first light snow had fallen.

The horse had been there so often that he automatically headed for the bottom field when we left the road. I stopped the horse to view the trap site.

Suddenly I realized something had just happened there! I jumped off the horse and raced to the trap. The leaves and the snow were torn up. The trap lay on its side, tripped. The cat had been in the trap. It had left some fur, and tore up jack getting out. It either stepped on the trap too lightly or the trap was too slow. After pulling loose, the cat had made for the creek in great long leaps in the snow. It crossed the creek on a log drift. I followed it through the heavy underbrush and lost the tracks on the other side. I searched in vain for more tracks and finally gave up the cause.

I could picture the cat laying up in the fork of a tree licking a sore foot and glaring down at me. It had beaten me. I would let it go. Perhaps we would meet again. That never happened.

A Close Call

They say your whole life will pass in front of you when you get in a dangerous situation. Maybe that's so, but this time I was telling myself, "Walter you've had some close ones, but you're going to get bitten this time!"

I was staring eyeball to eyeball with a good sized copperhead. It was a Mexican stand off. I could hear the dog coming up the fence toward us and I knew what would happen when he arrived.

I should have been more careful that morning. The dog and I had started toward the creek bottoms for a squirrel hunt. We reached the pasture fence, and following good safety procedure, I set my rifle down on the other side and went about twenty feet up the fence to crawl through.

Then, I saw it. It was perfectly camouflaged in the brown oak leaves that had come to rest against the bottom of the fence. It was directly under me. The repulsive, sickening sweet odor of a disturbed copperhead reached me.

I was between the lower strands of the barbed wire and the top of the woven wire. My right foot was on the ground and my left leg and foot were suspended across the

A Close Call

woven wire. My hands were on the fence pushing it down. My head and shoulders were already through.

I hung there frozen in position staring down at the copperhead. The pits were there on the sides of its snout. The darker hourglass markings were easily discerned on its bronze skin. It was flattened out and kinked for a strike.

I had always known as much as I traveled in the woods and creek bottoms that snake bite was a risk. Copperheads were numerous in the scrub timber and sandstone bluffs. More than an occasional cottonmouth showed up along Clear Creek.

A few close calls sharpened my skills enough that I was able to avoid contact, until now!

The dog had gone down the fence in the other direction to a familiar hole he used to get through. Now he was coming back up the fence on the copperhead's side. I knew that when the dog got there all heck would break loose.

I gathered my courage, threw myself back, and rolled away when I hit the ground. The snake struck, or at least moved when I did, but it didn't reach me.

The dog saw the snake and went for it. The snake struck him and the dog yelped. He grabbed the snake in his teeth, shook it, and with a snap of his head threw it in the air. The snake's body flew over the fence into the open pasture on my side. I scrambled for the rifle to finish the copperhead off. My hands were shaking so that it took several shots before I nailed it.

The dog was already feeling the effects of the bite. He had been bitten before and survived. I figured he would this time too, although he was getting very sick. We started for home. I tried to carry him but he wouldn't let me.

When we reached the house he found a cool shady place under a lilac bush and stayed there for two or three days, his head and neck swollen. My sisters and I offered him fresh milk and bacon grease. That was supposed to be a home remedy for snake-bitten dogs.

He wouldn't eat for several days. Then the swelling started to recede, he began eating, and was soon back chasing squirrels and living a normal dog's life.

My parents knew the dog was suffering from snake bite. My mother made the comment that she wished he would leave the things alone. I didn't tell them how he got bit or about my close call. I was afraid they would put a stop to our squirrel hunting.

People are skeptical when I mention the pungent odor that a disturbed copperhead will sometimes emit. I leave them to their own opinion. I smelled it that day when we went eyeball to eyeball in the fence row. On at least two other copperhead encounters I have experienced that sickening odor. If you have smelled it you know what I mean. If you have not smelled it, I hope you never do.

The Town Kids

BOOM, BOOM, BOOM! The shotgun blasts echoed along the creek bottom. Someone was really burning powder. The cadence of the shots was slow and deliberate. I doubted that it was rabbit hunters or squirrel hunters. One thing for sure, after all that racket the squirrels would be holed up for hours.

It was coming from down on the creek near the big pile of driftwood below Todd's Ford. The squirrels could wait. I opted to see who was making all the racket. I slipped into the underbrush and crept along to the bank of the creek in true Pathfinder fashion. Whoever the shooter was, I wanted to see him before he saw me.

There were two of them, boys about my age. They had scavenged a bunch of bottles and cans from the drift and were blasting away at them with an obviously new shotgun.

I squatted on the bank behind them, counting the spent shotgun hulls at their feet and mentally adding up the cost. After a few minutes one of them turned and spotted me. "Hey, how long you been there?" he asked gruffly. Perhaps he was a little frightened.

"Just a few minutes. Heard your shooting from up the

creek a ways," I said, trying to put him at ease. "Where are you from?" I asked.

"We're from town," the blond one answered.

"How did you get way out here?" I asked.

"We followed the railroad tracks," he said.

"Gosh that's a long way," I replied.

"I got a new shotgun and we were looking for rabbits. We haven't seen any. We're doing a little target practice before we start back. Want to try your luck?" he asked as he eyed my old .22 Winchester pump.

"Nope, don't want to waste my shells," I said. I couldn't believe that someone would target practice with a shotgun.

"Aw, you probably can't hit anything," he continued.

"Can too! I can knock squirrels out of tree tops," I said.

"All right, let's see you hit that top bottle then," he said. "If you miss it, I'll shoot it."

I eased back the hammer, took careful aim, and missed. Humiliated, I quickly chambered another cartridge and shot a second time. The bottle burst into pieces before he could shoot.

"Well," he said. "It took two tries, but I guess you hit it."

"You want to try?" I asked, holding the .22 out to him. "A rifle is a little different than a shotgun."

"No, think I'll stay with the shotgun," he grinned.

We introduced ourselves and I walked back to the railroad tracks with them. I invited them to come out again and I would show them where the rabbits were.

They never returned that I know of. The face and name of one left me long ago, but I remember the owner of the shotgun.

When I started high school in town we became friends. Not close friends, he was a town kid and I was a country kid, but we always had respect for one another.

He died an untimely death a few years ago. I'll always remember him as the kid with the new shotgun, target practicing on the banks of Clear Creek.

Who Believes a Kid?

The evening chores were almost finished. I still had to pump water for the black mare. It was easier and a lot more fun to ride the mare to the back pasture spring. I put her bridle on and hopped on her bare back. The evening quiet had set in. The day creatures were making their final sounds as they settled in for the night and the night creatures were calling to each other as they prepared to go about their business. In the distance, a coyote yipped.

We arrived at the spring. The mare was taking long noisy pulls of water. I sat there on her warm back enjoying the last of the sunset. It was a peaceful setting. It was a perfect reward for a long day's work.

Suddenly, I realized the mare and I were not alone! A large coyote sat on its haunches a short distance up the hillside in front of us. Cold shivers ran up my spine. The coyote and I stared at each other for a long time, perhaps even a minute. Then it nonchalantly trotted off, stopping once to look back at me. As I watched it disappear over the hill, I wondered how many other coyotes were around. I figured for one seen there would be a half a dozen others. I began plans then, for a Saturday morning coyote hunt.

The coyotes were working on the Leghorn hens. It was a frequent occurrence to find the evidence of their kills in the pasture, or more commonly between the corn rows in the field. They always left a few white feathers and the gizzard. The presence of a gizzard always labeled it a coyote kill. I could not blame them, I did not like gizzards either.

Later that night at the supper table I related that I had seen a big coyote over at the spring. "It just sat there and looked right at me!"

"Too bad you did not have your gun. You could have shot it," my dad said.

"I am going to hunt for it tomorrow instead of going to town," I answered. Whoops, my mother's antenna went up and dad and I both were on shaky ground.

"Now John, you know better than to say something like that. He listens to too many of his grandfather Cole's hunting tales anyhow," she explained.

"He won't want to miss a Saturday morning trip to the library and the afternoon picture show," Dad replied. He thought that would persuade me.

He was wrong, I had my plans for that coyote. A trip to town was a treat for a 1950's era farm boy and I did hate to miss it. My mind was set on going after the coyote. In the end they let me do it.

My dad was not a hunter. He always claimed he never had time. He did hunt pheasants when we lived out in the plains country. He never discouraged me from hunting. He bought the old model 1906 Winchester .22 for me when I was eight or nine years old. I was extra cautious with it and earned his trust.

My choice of firearms that Saturday was limited. I discovered that I only had shorts for the .22 and I knew they would not do the job. Dad's single barrel shotgun with its broken shell extractor would have to do. I took a pocketful of the heaviest loads. They were high brass, number six shot, pheasant and duck loads. They would have to do. I went to the lean-to on the barn where the tools were kept and found a sixteen penny nail. I beat the point of the nail flat with a hammer and dropped it into my coat pocket. I would use it to pry spent hulls from the gun.

The dog fell in behind and we went over the hill to

where I had last seen the coyote. The hunting ground was about forty acres of prairie and sedge grass. A few dry washes, and patches of buckbrush and briars made it an excellent cover for coyotes and small game. The chances of even laying an eye on a coyote were slim. But with a kid's blind optimism I began my hunt. I started on the outer edge and worked in, walking in circles, gradually closing into the center. I walked all morning and into the afternoon with the dog beside me.

We jumped both quail and rabbits, but we were coyote hunters that day. I was almost to the center when I saw a flash of gray up on the slope in a patch of persimmon sprouts and buckbrush. At first I dismissed it as a bird, but then I decided to check it out…

I walked into the edge of the knee-high brush and a coyote jumped up in the center of the patch not a dozen feet away. It was moving out. I jerked the shotgun up and got on the coyote just as it cleared the brush. The coyote's head was down and all I could see over the barrel was its rear end. I knew that I had to get it while it was close, so I shot. The force of the blast carried its rear end up. The coyote turned a cartwheel and came up on its feet, nipping at its tail.

I groped for the nail and tried to remove the expended shell. I fumbled. It seemed like an eternity. The dog charged in. The coyote broke away and started running. The dog was yipping at his heels. By the time I got the gun reloaded, the coyote and the dog were a long way off. I watched helplessly as they disappeared into a distant cornfield.

I ran after them and tracked them through the soft dirt of the cornfield. The coyote's tracks told me it was hit hard. I came out into the road and found the dog coming back to me.

We followed the blood sign across the road into a neighbor's pasture and lost it again. We walked back and forth across the pasture, but could not pick up a trail again. The dog and I were tired. We started homeward. Home was a place you could always go, to find solace and something to eat.

When we reached the house I helped myself to a plate of leftover biscuits, throwing the dog a couple. I was working on a second glass of milk when the folks and my sisters got home from town.

"How did the hunt go?" my dad asked.

"I shot it, but it got away," I answered. "I could not get the empty out. The coyote is crippled. I knocked it down. The dog and I tracked it. I think he went into Newt's lower field."

My dad grinned and said, "come on coyote hunter, we have chores to do."

But, the story does not end there...

A few days later, I was sitting on the loading dock at the Portia store feed room. I sipped my Double Cola and listened as a couple of area farmers were talking about how plentiful coyotes were getting.

"I found one dead in the field between me and Newt's the other day. He had his rear end all shot up with bird shot. Somebody must have caught him coming out of a chicken coop, I guess."

"I shot it," I said. "I followed it as far as Newt's place and lost the track."

"Yeah, sure you did." He winked at the other guy.

I gave up and turned my attention to my soda pop. With a smile of satisfaction, I thought, "Me and the dog, we know. We done good."

Who cares? After all, who believes a kid?

Watermelon and a Good Cigar

"Here," he said, holding out a cigar. "You furnished the watermelon, I'll furnish the cigars."

"Where did you get 'em?" I asked.

"They are my dad's, he's got a whole box of them."

So began one of the events that would make that day worth remembering many years later...

It was a sunny, perfect, late summer day in Clear Creek

country. We had got together that Saturday about mid-morning to start our day's agenda off with a squirrel hunt.

Rich had ridden his horse from his place a mile or two away. He had his rifle with him and was sporting a new pair of logger heel, lace-to-the-toe boots.

After hunting for a place in the shade, we tied his horse to the barn lot fence. I retrieved the old Winchester pump rifle from the house and we ambled on toward the first patch of timber.

The dog treed a squirrel in a large hickory tree at the head of a rocky draw. The squirrel was plainly visible. We debated who would shoot it out. Finally we both shot. Then we argued over which one of us connected with the target. Rich was the best shot, but I was not about to admit it. The owner of the squirrel still disputed, we moved on. The dog treed the next squirrel in a medium-sized oak with lots of limbs and leaves. We circled the tree several times, viewing it from different angles, and still could not find the squirrel. The dog wouldn't give up. He knew the crafty old bushy tail was up there.

"Rich, we've got to change our strategy. That squirrel is keeping the tree trunk between him and us. One of us needs to stand perfectly still and the other should take the dog around to the far side and raise a ruckus. That old squirrel will forget about the guy that's standing still and come around in view."

"Sounds right. Who's gonna do the shooting?"

"I will," I said, "since you claim you shot the other one. It's my turn."

"Aw shucks, you'll miss it!"

"Aw shucks," I mimicked. "I won't either."

Rich gave in and took the dog around to the other side. The ruse worked perfectly. The squirrel popped around on my side and I nailed it.

On up the hollow, we treed squirrel number three in a tall hickory. "It's my turn," Rich said and quickly potted the squirrel. The squirrel hung up in a fork in the tree about twenty feet above ground.

"Aw shucks. Who's gonna climb up after it?" Rich asked.

"Aw shucks. You shot it."

We solved the problem by throwing a barrage of rocks at the dead squirrel to dislodge it.

We were nearing the watermelon patch. We had planned it that way. We placed the guns and the squirrels on the grass under a shade tree and walked out into the melons.

We ran our hands over them, checked stems, and thumped them with thumb and forefinger. It was a ritual meant to show who had the most expertise in selecting ripe watermelons. Finally, we selected a large melon each, retreated to the shade tree and broke out our pocket knives. We ate, gorging ourselves, bantering, boasting, and telling jokes.

Full of watermelon, we stretched out in the shade in perfect contentment. Then Rich came up with the cigars... We lit up and puffed away. "Man, this is the life," I offered.

"Yup, this is living like a man ought to. You can't beat a good sweet watermelon."

"Or a good, sweet cigar," I added, drawing deep. The lively talk changed to wise and worldly comments becoming two cigar smoking gentlemen.

The cigar was a little more than half finished when I began to get an uncomfortable feeling in the pit of my stomach. Rich had stopped talking. I put the cigar out and laid there for awhile with a growing feeling of uneasiness.

"Rich, don't you think we better start back?"

"Yes, I guess so."

We got up and headed for the pasture fence. When we reached the fence I leaned over the top wire and started retching.

Rich immediately started to upchuck, too.

"It's those cigars," I gasped.

"Cigars don't make me sick. I was all right until you started vomiting all over the place."

We sat down under a nearby tree until the nausea ceased. By the time we walked back across the pasture we were feeling better, but Rich's new boots were really hurting him.

We scrounged up a pair of old tennis shoes for him and rested some more. We decided that what we needed was a soda pop from Portia store.

We were tired of walking. My horse was out in the pasture, so we decided to ride his mare double. Rich saddled the mare and mounted up. I handed him his unloaded rifle and the boots. He tied the boot laces together and hung the boots around his neck.

I was carrying Rich's field-dressed squirrels in a paper sack. The mare was skittish. She wouldn't let me get on behind Rich. We wrestled with the mare for several minutes. Rich, struggling with the reins and rifle, was telling her in no uncertain terms what kind of horse she was.

Finally, we arrived at a surefire strategy. I would climb upon the fence plank. Rich would ride the mare by and I would jump on behind with the squirrels. It worked, for a few seconds...

The mare came unglued. We lasted about three jumps and I went off, pulling Rich off with me. We landed in a pile: gun, squirrels, boots, and boys in the dirt.

The mare took off down the road. I jumped up and ran after the horse, trying to catch her. She had her fill of us and was heading for home. My choice cuss words just hurried her along.

I stopped and looked back. Rich was still lying on the ground. I ran back yelling, "Rich are you all right?"

Rich sat up. He was covered with dirt. The boots were still dangling around his neck. His baseball cap was tipped to the off side. "Aw shucks," he said, grinning from ear to ear. "I would have ridden her if you hadn't pulled me off. Anyway, it looks like we are walking."

That's the way Rich was, always ready for a good natured argument and always game.

Time clouds the memory and I can't remember if we got to Portia store for our soda pop or how Rich got back home.

Life taught some subtle lessons that day. We had so much fun learning.

In retrospect, what better to help the growing up process along, than a lively squirrel hunt with a good friend, topped off with watermelon and a good cigar?

The Open Well

It snowed that night and for awhile in the morning. It was a soft wet snow at least six inches deep. It was Sunday, I think, and things were slow around the farmstead. By afternoon, the dog and I were getting bored. It was a good time to go rabbit hunting. We followed the road down and around in the direction of Clear Creek, looking for rabbit tracks in the fresh snow.

On the road to Bud Todd's ford, we picked up a trail of tracks and jumped a rabbit a little further on. It ran west across the road and into a flat area of scrub oak, briars, and brush. Dad did not rent that particular property and I was not very familiar with it.

The dog pursued, barking as he went. I stepped through the dilapidated fence and followed. The dog cornered the rabbit in a snow-covered brush pile. Barking and circling, the dog tried to go in. Then he backed off and waited for me stomp the pile and kick the rabbit out as we had done many times before at other places.

I climbed up on the pile and started jumping up and down. I heard the sound of ice and sticks splashing water.

Looking down, I could see blue water. The only time I have jumped further and moved faster was when I stepped on a Kansas rattler. But that's a story for another time.

Cautiously examining the brush pile, I found it was covering an old dug well without a top on it. The brush pile had been placed there as a makeshift covering. It was rotting away, a waiting death trap.

The next day my dad set four posts and constructed a fence around it. I was probably twelve or thirteen years old, but I have never forgotten that close call and the safety lesson learned.

Midnight Saves a Jersey

Dad was struggling with a stubborn hitch pin on the tractor drawbar while I maneuvered the tractor forward or back at his command. The ice, snow, and slush did not make the task any easier. From my vantage point on the tractor seat I announced that our neighbor, Mr. Hicks, was coming up the lane. Dad kicked the offending pin loose and dropped the feed wagon tongue.

We watched the old gent's hurried approach. Something was wrong. He was wet from the waist down. His burned-out old stub pipe was bobbing up and down under his mustache.

"John!" he hollered. "I need help! One of my Jerseys fell through the ice on the creek. Can you bring your tractor and help me get her out?"

Dad grabbed a chain and with Mr. Hicks and me riding on the drawbar, we crossed the road and he drove to the pasture. He stopped the tractor at the top of the long snow-covered incline and we made our way down to the creek on foot.

The cow was in the middle of a shallow bend of Clear

Creek, just below a deeper hole. A cave off of the steep bank had formed a small landing at the water's edge. A narrow trail along the creek bank led to the landing. The cow's tracks showed she had followed this trail. From the landing she went out onto the ice and broke through. The old man had broken the ice out to her and tried to coax her to the bank. The cow had sulled and his efforts had been in vain.

She was down in two to three feet of water with outstretched head and neck just above the surface. Dad surveyed the situation and noted that it would be impossible to get near the creek with the tractor.

Turning to me Dad said, "Go get Midnight and bring that new rope."

Hicks was skeptical. "A horse will spook her. My cows aren't used to horses."

"We can try," Dad said. "A horse is about all that will save her."

Midnight was a super animal. One of those horses that you go through life comparing other horses against. Dad had peered intently into a sale barn pen of horses and after awhile announced, "That black mare is a good horse." He bought her that day and she served us well for many years...

I rode the horse down the path onto the landing and dismounted. Dad checked the saddle cinches and backed her to the water's edge. He dropped a loop over the Jersey's picture perfect set of horns and secured the rope to the saddle horn in a dally hitch so I could pull on the loose end and take up slack in the rope.

Still worried, Hicks was afraid we would break the cow's neck. "As long as we have a straight pull, she will take all the rope will," Dad reassured him. He tied the reins and dropped them over Midnight's neck. Wading out to the cow, Dad clucked to the horse and started shouting orders: "Git-up, whoa, back, back. Take up the slack!" The mare did it all on my dad's voice commands, time and time again. The cow was pulled toward the bank a few feet at a time. Standing at the shoulder of the horse, I dallied up the slack each time. Finally the cow was on solid ground.

We used feed sacks to rub her dry. After awhile she made a try at getting up. Finally the cow got her rear in the air and lunged to her feet. Completely lacking in gratitude, the cow snorted, lowered her head, and charged the mare. The mare neatly side stepped and whirled to face her adversary ready for the next move.

The cow trotted along the path and we followed her up the hill. The old man was profuse in his appreciation and praise of the horse.

At the top of the hill, I mounted again and waited for Dad to start the tractor. He set the throttle and went around in front to crank the engine. After several gut-wrenching pulls on the crank, it finally started. I knew why he liked his horses.

The Mailman's Lecture

The dog would not leave the tree. I turned the horse around and went back.

The weather had turned cool that September Saturday. It was a good day to explore. We were traveling up a timbered draw that meandered on down to Clear Creek. The ground and underbrush were still wet from the early morning rain.

We had passed a large oak snag. Its huge form stood out against the background of smaller trees. It was broken off about twenty feet above ground. Looking it over, I could tell it was hollow where it had broken. It had been in its present state a long time. The jagged edge of the break was weathered and gray. The tree was long dead and the bark was loosening.

The dog kept looking up and barking. He was telling me that something was up there. I rode close and examined the trunk's surface. There were claw marks on the trunk. Dismounting, I picked up a rock and beat on the tree. Nothing happened. I tried to call the dog away, but he refused to give up the idea that something was up there.

"All right," I said to the dog, "there had better be something up there." I really did not want to climb it, but I tied the horse to a nearby sapling and looked the tree over. I decided to throw my rope over a large, broke-off limb a few feet from the top. After several tries, I dropped a loop over the limb stub.

I tied a leather thong on the rifle, slung the gun across my back and started up the snag. It was difficult going until I reached the first limb. It did not get much better after that. I worked through broken limbs and a split in the trunk. Finally, I reached the top and cautiously peered over the edge. There was enough fur in that hollow tree to make a raccoon coat. Six pairs or more of angry eyes peered up at me. They all started to leave at once in a mad scramble up the sides to the top.

I dropped back down and found secure footing on the limb the rope was on. The first coon came over the top above me and I picked him off easily. Now the challenge was to reload. I wedged the forearm slide in the crook of my left arm, pinning it there. I shoved the rifle forward and then pulled it back, successfully reloading. I managed to shoot another one on its way down. The rest of the raccoons were on the ground running in all directions. The dog was going crazy. I quickly dropped down astraddle of the rope limb and shot two more on the ground.

I descended and collected my kill. I tied one pair together by their hind feet and then second pair by their hind feet.

The horse was a little nervous when I first approached him. I slung one pair in front of the saddle and the second pair behind the saddle. After they were in place he accepted the situation and I mounted up. I slung the rifle across my back.

I began to count the money as the horse made his way to the road. Understand, I admit to some primeval hunting instinct, but the main reason for hunting the fur bearing animals was money.

Cash on a marginal southwest Missouri farm during the early 1950's was scarce. Oh, there was enough to get by.

No allowances though. The money for small extras was doled out carefully. Ten cents for a soda pop or an occasional ice cream cone, and a Saturday afternoon movie cost another dime. A box of fifty rifle shells cost forty-five to fifty cents at the hardware store. A haircut cost fifty cents to a dollar depending which shop you went to.

Coon hides brought from two and a half to five dollars each. With four raccoons in the bag, I thought I was rich. I could picture that hunting knife that I pined for. Perhaps a rod and reel to replace my old hickory pole and bottle cork bobber.

The sound of the mailman's jeep jogged me out of my daydream. He stopped beside me and stared at the dead coons. "What have you got there?" he asked.

"Four of them, I spooked them out of an old hollow tree," I bragged.

"Is that so. I guess you know that the raccoon hunting season does not start for almost two months?"

"Yeah. Well I reckon the hides will keep," I said defensively.

"They will be blue. You will not get anything for them," he continued. "You probably wasted half of the coon population over several acres. Son, have you heard of the word sportsmanship?" I did not answer. I sat there embarrassed. He poured it on. "You messed with their den tree. That is illegal."

"It wasn't a den tree and I only climbed it," I sullenly retorted.

"Just the same, you better not let the game warden catch you. He is working in this area, I saw him down the road a few days ago." With that he put the jeep in gear and went on.

His stinging rebuke hurt and scared me. I left the road immediately and headed across country for home. I skinned the coons out and stretched the hides by nailing them to the inside of the rear barn wall. My dad spotted them a few days later and I got the mailman's lecture all over again.

They were right. Instead of the plush fur and light cream color inside of a prime hide they were a bluish white on the inside and were almost worthless. There are reasons for laws and regulations. Since that time I have hunted raccoon and squirrels, I have kicked up more than a few coveys of quail and I have walked the turkey woods. Through the years I have watched the sun come up on an assortment of marshes, rivers, and duck ponds across the state of Missouri.

With eighty points in the sack, I have watched over the gun barrel as a lone canvasback winged low over the decoys…and let it go. I have sat with my gun in my lap as an evening flight of woodies dropped in all around the boat a few minutes past shooting hours.

"Son, have you heard of the word sportsmanship?"

It is strange how a few choice words, said at the right time, will stay with you.

The Day I Heard Joe Swear

Shocking corn fodder is hot, hard, and miserable work. But, back then it was just part of living. As soon as the ears of corn began to mature, the stalks were harvested by an ingenious machine that cut the stalk off a few inches above the ground. The machine was drawn by horses or a tractor. It did not matter what the manufacturer called the machine. We just called it a binder. While being pulled, the binder would gather loose stalks of corn and bind them into a bundle with twine, dropping them out on the ground behind it. The bundles probably weighed forty pounds, more or less. The bundles of corn were left where they fell to cure and dry in the hot August sun for a few days.

It was the shocker's job to pick up the bundles and build a tepee-shaped shock, the outer layers protecting the inner layers. It made a durable semi-weatherproof storage device. The ears of corn were later removed from the stalk by hand, and the stalk and cured leaves were fed to the livestock.

At age fifteen I began hiring out to area farmers to shock corn or put up hay. It brought a much needed extra few dollars. This day I was working for Joe. Now, Joe was one of the nicest of people. Devout and even-tempered, he was just a great guy to be around. Joe would never use a swear word.

That day we were working in a field of Joe's corn just east of Oak Ridge Schoolhouse. We had finished setting a row of shocks down one side of the field and were working our way back up toward the other end and the fence row next to the road. It was hot. We were dusty and thirsty.

It was a time before commercial water jugs, and if there were commercial jugs, nobody in the Portia community used them. Most farmers simply took an empty glass vinegar jug and wrapped an empty burlap bag around the clean gallon jug. The jug was filled with well water and capped. The burlap bag was given a thorough soaking. The evaporation process then kept the water fairly cool most of the day.

That day, Joe had set our jug of water in the shade of a fencepost and the buckbrush growing in the fence row. Halfway across the field, we could see the jug and we both were talking about how good that water would taste when we got there. We paused from our work to rest a bit. Just then the neighbor's big old friendly stock dog came ambling down the fence row. When he got to the water jug he hiked up a back leg and did to that jug what city dogs do to fire plugs.

Joe let out a bellow and reminded that dog of his parentage. Perhaps a bit embarrassed by his out of character cuss word, Joe turned to me and said, "Did you see that? He salted down our water jug!"

Joe solved the problem by going home and getting a fresh jug of water. Instead of setting it by the fencepost this time, he hung it on the fencepost. "There," he said. "He isn't that tall."

Home Again Safe and Sound

It felt awkward riding the horse in my school clothes. They were certainly not the clothes or shoes I usually wore while riding the horses. The horse sensed something different, too. He walked with an uncertain step, hesitating when I turned him down the back road toward Clear Creek. It was dusk, we were leaving home and heading across country to town.

I had a transportation problem and as usual the horse provided the solution. I was a freshman in high school now and I wanted to attend the basketball games. My folks did not have the time or the gasoline to waste running me to the ball games.

There was an old abandoned overgrown roadway that ran across Clear Creek and intersected the main road about a mile west of town. The old settlers had went to great lengths to construct a ford across Clear Creek. I discovered it during the drought when the water in the creek was very low. The builders had rowed up huge boulders across the creek and filled in behind with smaller rocks and gravel. It had been there for decades, maybe even since the mid 1800s. During normal times, water was about eighteen inches deep over the ford. The hole created below the boulders on the downstream side was five or six feet deep. It was still a solid ford and it was my own shortcut to town. The horse and I had explored and even trapped along the deserted and washed out roadway.

It was my plan to ride the horse into town and slip through some back streets to the school. I would tie him to the rear ball diamond fence near the railroad tracks. It worked well for a couple of times.

I would leave the game a few minutes early and was out of town before the post ballgame traffic started. I am sure more than one person puzzled over the horse and rider that slipped past the streetlights.

On our third trip, I left the game early as planned, to find that clouds had closed in and it was as dark as the inside of a boot. The horse knew his way and we made it fine until we reached the Clear Creek ford. The horse misjudged and we went over on the deep end.

Now, the horse and I had been swimming in Clear Creek many times, but not in the dark with his saddle on and me fully clothed. I hung on and he swam to the waters edge and lunged up the bank. He shook the excess water off and we went home cold and wet. I slipped him into the barn and dried him and the saddle off the best I could with a dry saddle blanket.

I slipped in the side door of the house and met the usual

query from the folks bedroom, "Walter, is that you?"

"Yep, home again safe and sound." I did not mention I was wet. To this day I don't know if they ever knew about my late night dunking in Clear Creek.

The next trip to the ballgame would be my last trip on horseback...

It was halftime and a group of us were at the concession stand in the main hall waiting for the game to restart. The outside hall door burst open and one of the town rowdies came racing in. "Hey! There is a horse tied to the ball diamond fence! Somebody has ridden it to the ballgame. Who does it belong to?" the kid asked.

I kept silent, wondering what was going to happen. I didn't have to wait long.

"Let's go let it loose and have some fun," one of them chirped. They headed towards the door.

I knew I had to do something fast. In an attempt to stall them, I called after them, "Wait a minute guys, those things are dangerous. They will hurt you. I heard of one biting a guy's ear off."

"Aw I don't believe that," one jerk said.

"Sure, they kick like heck, too! You know how old Abe Lincoln's head looks so warped in all the pictures? They say that a horse kicked him and caved his head in. He almost died from the injury. True story," I said.

They hesitated, considering what I had said. "Well," one clown cracked, "I would sure hate to look like Abe Lincoln." They gave up and went back into the gym.

The game started again and I went out to check the horse. He nuzzled me as if to say this isn't for us, lets get out of here. I put the bit in his mouth, tightened the girth and mounted up.

My heart was heavy with a disappointment. Making the transition from a one room country school to a high school in town had opened my eyes to another world. I had already found out how cruel teenagers could be to each other. The carefree days of roaming the Clear Creek bottoms were gone. Later those days would become treasured memories. In fact, my whole world was about to change drastically...

This would be the last time for the horse. If I rode him back again, those kids would turn him loose or even hurt him. It was only a matter of time. The horse and I struck First Street and headed north. Turning west on Spring Street Road, the horse eased into his comfortable ground-covering running walk. We were home in no time.

"Walter, is that you?"

"Yep, home again, safe and sound."

...Author's Notes...

A cabin...

The lane I followed in Home Again Safe and Sound lead to the creek ford, and came out west of Clear Creek at what is now called Katy Lane. Just southwest of there, around the hill and at its base, was a large old log cabin. The cabin had been turned into a barn, with sheds added on three sides. The floor and loft had been removed, although their anchoring notches in the logs were clearly evident. My family rented the farm for extra farming ground and pasture. I worked at storing hay in the barn, including the log cabin part. I was fascinated by the cabin. It had a definite sense of history about it.

Years later while doing history research in a Columbia, Missouri library, I ran across a Vernon County history book with a description and location of the first residence constructed in Clear Creek Township. I believe it may have been that cabin.

Oak Ridge School students about 1953.

Oak Ridge, Missouri

First row (from left to right): Raymond Yakel, June Corder, Joan Ryan, Jeannie Allen, Billy Gross. Second row: Alma Horning, Jimmy Gross, Mary Ryan, Helen Yakel, Kenneth Horning. Third row: Ella Mae Jackson, Walter Ryan (me), Neil Hoffman, Miss Annie Alexander our teacher, and Nancy Corder.

Richard Jackson was absent that day. Or he may have been taking the picture. Neil Hoffman and I were in the eighth grade. Oak Ridge School was located on what is now EE highway. It was one half mile west of Portia store. The Oak Ridge School building still exists as a farmer's hay barn.

Posing before the festivities

Schell City, Missouri

First row (from left to right): Raymond Yakel, Kenneth Horning. Second row, Helen Yakel and Alma Horning. Walter Ryan on Midnight.

Country schools were invited to the parade and festivities at Schell City Missouri. There were bikes, doll buggies, and costumes. I rode Midnight the horse twelve miles (one way) to participate. Some of my Oak Ridge schoolmates pose with us. Midnight gave many rides that day. The date was probably 1952.

My final days at Clear Creek . . .

Tragedy struck our family during my Freshman year of high school. Our mother became ill with cancer. After a heroic but terrible two year battle, she passed away. I will always remember the kindness of the good people of the Oak Grove Baptist Church and the Portia community. My father was exhausted, demoralized and devastated. We could no longer carry the debt load and were about to lose the farm. I dropped out of high school near the end of my Junior year and took a job.

One day a stranger from Kansas City drove into the driveway. He wanted to know if the farm was for sale? The man related that he had lived in the community at one time and he had always wanted that farm. He explained that he had recently came into some money and he made dad a generous offer. It was more than enough to pay the debt off.

A friend working with me had previously related that his grandmother had an old out-of-the-way timbered farm for sale. We bought it, and Dad, my two younger sisters, and I moved near the Sac River area in eastern Cedar County. My employer encouraged me to go back to school. They allowed me to work after school and at night while I finished high school.

I have always worked. I have never been without a

job for more than a day. I have picked up some college hours along as I worked. I have lived long and had a good career. I have met a lot of fine people and had some amazing experiences along the way.

Those years working and playing along the prairie hills and the Clear Creek bottoms in Missouri remain a treasured memory along what I call my Sundown Trail.

ABOUT THE AUTHOR

Walt Ryan was born in Cheyenne County, Kansas. The first home he can remember was a sod-walled house located on a rise south of the Republican River. He attended his first eight years of school in one room school houses on the high plains and in the Missouri Ozarks. Ryan grew up with an appreciation for the people of the western frontier, then and now. He enjoys writing about them in fact and fiction.

Ryan has lived and worked in the plains country and traveled the West. As a youth, he worked as a combiner on the wheat harvest circuit beginning on the Waggoner Ranch in Texas, and finishing the season on the Rosebud Indian Reservation in South Dakota. When Walt Ryan writes of horses and cattle, he does so with first hand knowledge. Ryan's many work experiences include mill hand, long haul truck driver, newsletter editor, photographer, writer, electrician, and over the years he worked through the ranks at several consumer cooperatives.

Ryan's work has been published in the Ozarks Mountaineer, Rural Missouri Back Page, The Iron Men Album Magazine, Rural Missouri Guest Column, and various midwest publications. In addition to writing books and posting on his blog, he enjoys collecting antique firearms and horse gear. Ryan currently lives with his wife Denny in Mid-Missouri.

www.SundownTrailBlog.com

Made in the USA
San Bernardino, CA
02 August 2014